I0557186

An Heir for the Billionaire Werebears

Alyse Zaftig

Copyright © 2015 Alyse Zaftig

All rights reserved.

ISBN: 978-1634810289

Eviction

I looked at the paper in my hand and tried not to cry.

EVICTION it told me in bright red letters across the top.

I was homeless, now. My stuff was out on the curb. My pretty lace prom dress. My shoe collection that I was too poor to afford but had anyway. All of it was on the street.

Tears dripped silently down my face as I loaded up my trunk, back seat, and passenger seat with everything that I owned in the world. Sadly, my car wasn't even full. There was plenty of room for more stuff. Stuff I didn't have. I had sold my beloved guitar, the one that my dad gave me for my 16th birthday, last month in order to buy groceries.

Being poor sucked. I had a half gallon of gas, which I hoped would last me a while. Thank goodness my dad had had the foresight to buy me a fuel efficient Toyota.

He was also the reason that I was where I was.

I had grown up as a completely spoiled princess, with a dad whose credit card could fix anything. When I was 16, instead of making me use the gas credit card that I kept in my glove compartment, he would fill up my gas tank every week. He loved me.

College was more of the same. I'd skipped class a lot and never done my homework, but some slick words to the dean and a discreet donation of millions later, I was admitted to UCLA, his alma mater.

When he died during my second semester of college, we learned that he hadn't been able to afford to donate that much. He'd borrowed against his business, a calculated gamble that he thought he would win. He could earn back that much in the matter of months.

He was wrong. He died before he could.

That left my mom and me in some dire straits. We sold our house. Sold everything that we could. And in the end, we ended up at zero.

Mom had not been raised to deal with this, either. She had always been a pretty heavy drinker, and the death of my father and our subsequent debt problem drove her to drink even more. She lived in a tiny apartment in Thousand Oaks and was at the liquor store every day.

I couldn't live with her. She was in bad shape, and being

around her only made me worse. We were estranged at this point. She loved the bottle more than she loved her daughter.

I had appealed to the financial aid office, showing them that we could not afford to send me to school. The lady had been sympathetic, but rules were rules. I took a gap year, because I could not afford to pay for school.

It was a nasty shock to come home from UCLA and see an eviction notice on my door. Yeah, I knew that my landlord had been trying to contact me to get back rent, but I had dodged him neatly time and again. Or so I thought.

My eyes filled with tears, but I wiped them away. I could fall to pieces later, but I needed to figure out a plan now.

I got into my car, and I turned on the ignition. The warm air of my air conditioner blew on my face. For some reason, it was the straw that broke the camel's back. I buried my face in my hands and cried loudly, noisily. My sobs wracked my entire body, and I gasped for air as tears and snot ran from my face.

I heard a tap on the door.

"Are you ok, miss?"

A concerned citizen was out there. Oh gosh, he was so

handsome, with dark blond hair, kind deep blue eyes, and lightly gold skin. I wasn't hideous, but I was an absolute mess right now. I had never been a pretty crier, and I knew that I had to look my worst at the moment.

I rolled down my window. "I'm fine," I lied. "It's ok."

"What's going on?" he asked me. "Let me help."

I shook my head no. "I have to go."

I tried to roll up the window, but he stuck his hand in.

"I'm not a rapist or murderer," he said. "Seriously. Tell me what's going on."

"You asked for it." I glared at him. "I had to drop out of UCLA...well, stop out of UCLA...because my dad died and left us with millions in debt. I just got evicted from my apartment, and now I'm homeless in LA. I am going to try to find a 24-hour parking garage so that I am not on the street tonight. My car has everything that I own in the world." I was so humiliated, telling my private sorrows, my dirty laundry, to this complete stranger.

"So if you'll excuse me..."

"Wait a minute," the stranger said, his hand still in my window. "I think I can help you."

9

My tears, which had been slowly leaking down my face the entire time, stopped.

"You can?"

"Yeah," he said.

"What's in it for you?" I asked suspiciously. My dad did not raise any fools.

"Something that I think that you'd be ok with," he returned. "How about you follow me in your car? I'll cancel my meeting, and you can come home with me."

Sounded sketchy. "No, thanks."

"Hey," he said. "I know that you have to take a leap of faith. Look, here's my driver's license."

He reached into his back pocket and pulled out his ID. "Text my license number to someone you trust and tell them to sic the police on me if you disappear."

I needed this chance, however slim it might be. I took a picture of his driver's license, and I sent it to my best friend, Kara. "Ok." I heard the little sound my phone made when the picture was sent. "I'm game."

"Great." He smiled, and I almost fell backward in my seat. His teeth were strong, white, and straight. They flashed brilliantly. In a city with people who bleached their teeth, I could tell the difference between bleached teeth and naturally white teeth. His were natural. He looked like a wet dream with his high cheekbones and his dimples.

Someone so hot couldn't be a scary person, right? Yeah, he had a pretty fierce beard, but his eyes were kind.

I drove behind him, nervously checking my gas tank. The needle did not move much as we drove into Bel Air. He stopped at the gate of his community and said something to the guard. The guard waved at both of us to come in. He closed the gate after me.

Bel Air

My head felt like it was swiveling around. My dad had been fairly wealthy — we used to live in Malibu on the beach — but that was nothing compared to the opulence that I saw in Bel Air. These were not houses. They were extremely huge compounds. Some of the homes were gated so that you could not see them from the street, though others were free and clear. I could see the landscapers working on the huge yards. It was California, so they were not decorated with thirsty flowers.

"Don't you know there's a drought?" was the chorus when we saw people with living plants on their lawns.

Instead, they had cacti and some hardy desert plants that did not require a lot of water.

My humble little Toyota did not even remotely fit in here. I hunched over in my seat, making my body smaller. I was ashamed to be poor. Even when my parents had been wealthy, they had not been this wealthy.

I saw his car pull into a circular driveway. I pulled in after him. It was a pure white house that looked like the plantation houses in older movies about the South. It had big white columns.

I turned off my ignition, and I stepped out of my car.

I gave myself a mental pep talk.

"You're just as good as these people," I scolded. "You are the same as them. Everyone puts their pants on the same way in the morning."

I squared my shoulders and lifted my chin. I could do this.

I mentally imagined myself as an Ent from the Lord of the Rings, one of the giant trees that could talk. Yes, in real life I was a very petite, curvy woman. But I could pretend.

I marched up the driveway, and I went through the open garage door. He was waiting for me there.

"I'd like you to meet someone," he said, taking my arm and intertwining it with his.

I walked up the steps from the garage into the house, feeling a bit of sweat on the back of my neck. I wiped my spare palm on my jeans.

When we got in the house, I saw him cutting up some broccoli.

"Aren't you supposed to be in a meeting?" he asked without looking up. When he turned around, he blinked. I saw that he was a dead ringer for the man whose arm I was holding.

"You're twins." Oh god. I was Captain Obvious. My cheeks flushed. Oh god.

"Guilty," said the one in the kitchen. "And who are you?"

"I'm Zeva," I said, letting go of the first one's arm. "What's your name?"

"Xavier," he said, his eyes twinkling at me. "I'm so pleased to make your acquaintance. You smell very nice. What is it? Some kind of expensive floral perfume? It's perfect for you."

"No," I said. "I don't wear perfume."

"Oh." He paused. "Oh. That must be why you're here."

I frowned at him, totally confused.

"Would you like a drink?" the other one said chivalrously. "Do you want a Coke?"

"Sure," I replied. "I just realized that I don't know your name."

"Asher, honestly, where are your manners?" Xavier chided. "How could you meet a lovely lady like this one and not introduce yourself?"

"I got...caught up," Asher said. A silent moment of twin communication passed between them.

"I see," Xavier said, rubbing his matching beard.

"I don't. What's going on? Could you buy me a vowel?"

"Here's your Coke," Asher said, opening a literally cool drawer full of soda. It said 'SubZero' on it. He popped the tab and handed it to me. "Sit down. Let's talk."

"I'm not really sure what's going on either," Xavier said, his eyes flicking towards me. "So someone clue me in and bring me out of the dark."

"She's having a few problems. Zeva, why don't you tell Asher what happened today?"

"Um," I looked down at my feet.

"I just got evicted. And the financial aid office says that I won't qualify for aid, so I have to take a year off of school. I was planning on finding a 24-hour parking garage when your twin met me and brought me home. That's a pretty quick summary of my day."

"Where do you go to school, honey?"

I thought about protesting his use of 'honey', but I didn't. "I go to UCLA. Well, I went to UCLA."

"Interesting," Xavier said.

"Very," Asher added.

"You know, our dad is the one whose name is on the new UCLA stadium."

I gaped at Xavier. "Really?"

"Yeah. I think we could help you out."

"Help me out...like get me a scholarship?"

"Oh, I think we can do better than that."

They smiled at each other.

"We're going to tell you things that are private. Very private. Xavier, do you still have that NDA on file?"

"What's an NDA?"

"A non-disclosure agreement. You don't have to agree to the contract that we're about to give you, but you can't talk about the meeting we're having today. Is that ok?"

"I guess." I wasn't really in a position to dictate terms. "That's fine."

Xavier put a non-disclosure agreement in front of me. Asher highlighted several places.

"Just sign where it's highlighted."

I signed and initialed all the pages.

"Ok. What are you two up to?"

"We are the head of an organization."

"What kind of organization?" I was regretting coming into their house, and I wondered if I could get out before they could catch me.

Probably not. They looked pretty fit, and I ran about as fast as a turtle. A Galapagos turtle. There was that old saying that if you met a bear in the woods, you didn't have to outrun the bear. You just had to outrun the person next to you. I was always going to be the person next to you that got eaten by the bear.

"An organization of people like us. In order to solidify our position as leaders, we need to have children. We've been the head of this organization for almost 3 years now. If we don't have c— children within the next two years, we have to forfeit our position and our scumbag cousin will take over."

"What makes him a scumbag?"

"He is so sketchy." Xavier's fists were clenched. "We've never been able to pin anything on him, but there have been disappearances..."

"So you don't want him to take over. That would be really bad."

"That's right," Asher said, nodding. "You're right."

"So you want me to have your kids," I said, connecting the dots. "That's what this is about."

"I think we can solve each other's problems," Asher said. "You only need money. We need a kid. And we need a human."

"Uh, you say that like you're not human."

Offer

They only looked at me. I did the math.

"Oh my god!" I turned and sprinted for the door.

"Just wait," Asher told me.

"What are you guys?" I screamed. "Aliens? Is this an abduction? HELP!"

Asher's hand was on my mouth.

"We're not aliens. We're men. Mostly." Asher sighed. "We're werebears."

"Were-shifters don't exist. They're only for movies."

26

"Welcome to Hollywood, sweetheart," Xavier said, putting his big arm around my shoulders.

I blinked up at him. He was so tall, towering over me.

"Here's our offer." Xavier's extraordinary blue eyes with light blue lines in them met mine.

"We'll buy you a house. Well, first you'll move in with us for the coming year. We'll make a baby. In return, you get that house. You'll get your tuition and education completely paid for, whether you choose to get your LPN at a community college or your PhD at UCLA. We can help you out with getting back in. I assume you've already talked to their counselors."

I nodded.

"Superb. So that's the offer: house and education. Oh, and your medical expenses will be paid for life. You'll also get a stipend of $10,000 a month for the rest of your life. Do you think that's fair? Should we throw in a new car?"

My jaw was completely open. "That's a ferociously generous offer. What's the catch? I just have to have a baby?"

"You'll be sleeping with both of us, you know," Asher said quietly.

"That's a pro, not a con," I shot back.

Xavier's face lit up. "That's why

you are perfect for this."

"I'm in." I lifted my chin. "I can do this." I hope.

"Awesome," Xavier chirped. "Sign our contract."

I read it, and I signed where I needed to.

Xavier took it back from me. "Let me show you to your room."

I followed him up the staircase, which brought us to a very pretty room.

"This is the Rose Room. Our mom went overboard when she decorated it. It's in shades of rose. Do you like it?"

"Like it?" I asked in total disbelief. "I love it."

"Good," Xavier said. "Your closet is in here."

The closet was bigger than my former apartment. It was connected to a pretty marble bathroom with gold taps. All in all, the room was the nicest one I had ever been in. It was mine, all mine. Well, for the next year anyway.

"Wow."

"Asher and I have bedrooms that are around yours. You can sneak into our beds anytime. When you are fertile, we'll smell it."

"Smell it? Smell me? How?"

Xavier sighed. "We have an enhanced sense of smell."

"Oh." I nodded. "Okay."

"I can send movers over to your old apartment to help you get your stuff here."

I shook my head. "Weren't you paying attention earlier? I was evicted. All my stuff is in my car."

"Asher and I will help you bring it in."

"No," I said firmly. "There's no need to bring my furniture in here. I'll just take my suitcase. I'll be set."

"That reminds me. I need to give you a set of keys. Here, take mine." The key was an ornate old-time key. It had a bear engraved on it. Another button was attached to it, which I guessed went to the garage.

"These seem old."

"They are anything but. Turn the key head."

I twisted it in my hand. Inside, it glowed.

"Eek!" I yelped, dropping it to the floor. "Is it radioactive?"

"No," Xavier chuckled, picking up the key. "It's just bioluminescent bacteria. Your key can help you find your way in the dark. It's like a lodestone. It'll bring you home, wherever you are."

"That sounds awesome. What about GPS?"

Xavier raised a brow. "Do you know our address?"

I flushed. "No."

"There you go, then. I am going to get your suitcase, and then I'll be right back."

He wrapped me in a big hug, squeezing me tight. His arms were like steel bands around me, but I got the impression that he wasn't hugging me very hard. I sat down on my bed and hugged my knees. I didn't know what he thought he was doing, but he couldn't get into my car without my keys.

In less than a minute later, my suitcase was in my room, carried by a very cheerful Xavier.

"How did you even get in? My car was locked."

"Was is the operative word."

My keys were in his hand.

"Did you think that I hugged you just to snuggle?"

"You picked my pocket!" I gasped. "How could you!? I didn't even notice."

"I'm very, very good." He winked.

Suddenly, I was very conscious that this smoking hot werebear was in my room. His eyes were on mine, and he wasn't joking anymore.

After a few beats, he broke the moment by clearing his throat. "I'll be downstairs if you need me. Just settle in. Take a shower. Relax.

We'll get some dinner." He caught one of my hands and kissed it in an unexpectedly gallant gesture. "I'm glad that you're here." He left me in my room alone.

I stripped and went into my shower. I needed to wash off everything that had happened today, the highs and the lows. I stared at the tile wall as the water pounded down on me. This whole situation was surreal. First of all, I never knew that were-animals actually existed. I thought that werewolves were the stuff of horror movies and Twilight. Second, I was now apparently living with weres, and I had already agreed to bear their child, no pun intended, so that they could solidify their position. I shook my head and let the water wash away all of my racing thoughts.

When the bathroom mirror was completely steamed up, I got out of the shower and wrapped myself in a pink towel. I got dressed in one of my pretty dresses. Yeah, I was a bedraggled homeless person only a few hours ago, but the shower had me feeling brand new, like anything was possible. I had been given an opportunity, and I was determined to make the most of it. I put on a bit of makeup, just enough to make me not look like a hideous troll, and I went barefoot downstairs.

The scent of cooked meat permeated the air.

Dinner

"Smells good," I called. "What is it?"

"Come down," Xavier called. "Dinner is ready."

As I went, someone wearing a chef hat waved at me and was gone.

"Who was that?"

"We ordered a meal, but we told our chef that we wanted privacy. We gave him a 100% tip, so he was pretty happy to go."

My stomach grumbled. I hadn't even realized that I was hungry while I was in the shower, but smelling the food made me ravenous.

"What do we have?"

I looked at the table. It was practically groaning under the weight of all the food. There were potatoes, salad, and steak.My eyes popped out of my head.

"Holy cow!" My hand went over my heart. "That's so much food."

"We've got stuffed potato skins with caramelized Gruyère cheese, cream, green onions, garlic, and a little pepper. Try some. These are my favorite."

Without any kind of shame, Xavier quickly cut a piece and put it in my mouth.

"This is incredible," I said rudely with a full mouth. "Oh, my god." My mouth was bursting with the perfect medley of flavors. I had always liked potatoes, but this was next-level deliciousness.

"Try something lighter," Asher said. "Here." He stuck a fork in a romaine lettuce heart.

I chewed and swallowed. "What's even in this? It tastes like lemon."

"It's lemon zest dressing. Do you like it?"

"I love it," I said wholeheartedly. It was an understatement.

"Our main course is filet

mignon."

"Of course it is," I said, refraining from rolling my eyes. "Because there's nothing more typical of bears than eating cows."

Asher laughed. "I like steak, sweetie. They are prey. We are predators." He cut off a slice and offered it to me. The soft meat was perfectly seasoned with rosemary and some kind of butter sauce.

"If you feed me like this for an entire year, you are going to have to roll me out."

They only laughed. "Sweetheart, bear cubs take a lot of strength and energy. Believe me, you'll need all of this. Anyways, I wouldn't mind putting more curves on your delicious body. We've got triple chocolate brownies warming in the oven."

I shook my head. "I can just about handle one steak, but that's all you should expect from me."

"Don't worry," Xavier said, grinning. "We'll eat the rest."

I looked at their strong, tall bodies with their broad shoulders and toned upper arms. I believed it. It took a lot more fuel to run one of those than my more petite body.

I sat down and spooned up some stir-fried broccoli and shiitake mushrooms onto my plate. I took some of the salad, the smallest filet mignon, and a potato skin.

The boys fixed their own plates, and we all dug in. We didn't talk very much as we stuffed our faces with the delicious food fit for kings.

I knew that I could get used to eating like this.

At the end of dinner, when my plate was clean and the boys had polished off everything in the dishes on the table, Asher went to the oven. He pulled out a pan of brownies. They smelled absolutely divine.

I looked at it, put a hand on my stomach, and groaned.

"I can't eat another bite."

"That's fine," Xavier told me. "I can."

Asher took out a tub of vanilla gelato from the freezer. I watched in disbelief as they scarfed down the pan of brownies a la mode. If a normal human tried to eat that many calories, I am pretty sure that they would throw up. I know I would have if I had tried to match their pace during dinner.

In no time at all, the brownies and gelato were gone. Asher put everything in the sink.

"Our housekeeper comes in the morning. You'll meet her tomorrow."

"Okay."

My eyelids were beginning to drift downward. I was so full, and I had had a big day.

"You're falling asleep in your chair," Asher said fondly. He tucked a strand of hair behind my ear. "I'll take you to bed."

"I can walk," I protested, my voice muzzy. "I can do it."

"Allow me," Asher said. He picked me up tenderly, wrapping his arms around me, keeping me safe and secure. He took me up the stairs swiftly and steadily, staring into my face the whole time. His gorgeous face took my breath away.

When we got to the Rose Room, he put me down on the bed, turned down the covers, and then pulled me to the edge.

"Arms out."

If I were awake, I might protest, but it was hard to muster the will. I raised my arms. He took off my dress, unzipping me and pulling it off. Then he put me into my freshly turned down bed. The sheets were cool and smooth against my legs.

I should thank him. But somehow, sleep overtook me before I could.

Housekeeper

When I woke up, the sun was shining. There were birds chirping outside of my window. Assholes. I didn't want to be awake yet. I felt like I was part of a giant, fluffy cloud. I didn't want to move an inch. My eyes went around my room.

Where was I?

Yesterday came back. Right. I was in the Rose Room, not my own tiny little apartment.

I could smell something. It was like bacon. After a half second, I realized it was bacon.

I brushed my teeth, cleansed my face, and brushed my hair quickly. With a single coat of mascara, I pretended that I had on enough makeup, even though no girl in LA walked around bare-faced. There were too many perfect beach bunnies. I walked downstairs quickly.

"Good morning."

There was a matronly woman. She was loading the dishwasher with all the dishes and pans from last night.

She came to me, her hand out. "I'm Gaia. I'm their housekeeper. You must be the newest addition to the household."

I shook her hand. "I'm so pleased to meet you. Your breakfast smells great."

"Asher and Xavier have already eaten. Yours is on a plate in the toaster oven." She pulled out a heavy plate with bacon. There was an omelette on it.

"Is that spinach, mushroom, tomato, and feta? How did you know what I like?"

"Psychic." She winked at me.

"I think you really are," I said slowly. "There's no way that you could know this."

"It's a pretty useless gift, as far as talents go. If I could direct it, I would try to find tomorrow's lottery numbers." She laughed. "It just happens randomly that I'll know something with certainty. I'm glad you like it."

She squeezed some oranges right then and there to make me fresh juice, and then she took the plate to the table, which already had a fork and knife waiting. I dug in. She had put garlic and butter into these eggs. It made my favorite food even better than it normally was. I loved it. I loved her already, because she fed me awesome food. I ate slices of delicious bacon as the end of my meal, closing my eyes as I savored the salty crispness.

She was wiping down the counter. I rinsed my plate off in the sink, and I put it in the full dishwasher. I closed it. I couldn't find the start button.

"It's inside of the dishwasher," she said. "Here, let me."

She opened the dishwasher. There was a panel of buttons on top. She pressed start, and then she closed it.

"Wow," I said, blinking. "This house is so futuristic."

"You get used to it. Don't worry."

I shook my head.

"Do you know when Xavier and Asher will be back?"

"They come back after I leave. I leave around noon. I clean during the morning. If you have laundry, just drop it in the hamper in the laundry room. It's the first thing that I take care of after breakfast. Just put a note on something that should be dry cleaned, and I will take care of drop off and pick up at the dry cleaners. I have a debit card for household expenses."

"Sounds great," I said. "Thank you for breakfast. It was absolutely delicious."

She smiled at me. "Anytime."

I drifted upstairs and took out my computer. I had always been a big researcher, and now I needed to find out the best way to get pregnant.

There were forums upon forums filled with women who had fertility problems. I found so many horror stories. One woman talked about the expensive injections that she took over a long period of time in order to freeze her eggs. Facebook famously covered egg freezing for its employees, and it sounded like a great step forward. But as I read the accounts of these women, I realized that egg freezing wasn't as simple as people made it out to be. It was very expensive and took a lot of time. And you had no guarantees at the end that your egg would make a baby.

It looked like artificial insemination was a lot easier on a woman. You just had to check the time that you ovulated.

I started looking at when people ovulated. It was generally in the middle of their cycle. If you had a 4-week cycle, then it would be two weeks between periods.

I pulled up my period tracker on my iPhone and looked. That was today.

The fertile period was sort of up in the air. Some people said it was 12 hours. Others said that it was 36. I made a mental note to talk to the boys about it when they got home.

I closed my laptop and wandered around my new home. Besides the kitchen and my bedroom, I had not seen very much. I found a set of stairs going down, and I walked into Wonderland.

Wonderland

There are a lot of guys who turn their basements into Man Caves, with a big TV and a fridge full of beer. This Man Cave was on steroids.

They had a bowling alley down here. There was a pool table, a ping-pong table, and an air hockey table. I could see through a pair of French doors that they had an indoor swimming pool, which seemed smart with the Los Angeles sun. Mosaics covered the wall in there, telling the story of The Old Man and the Sea by Ernest

Hemingway, one of my favorites.

Another room had a movie theater. I guessed that this was the closest that they got to a prototypical Man Cave. It had surround sound speakers, and the screen wasn't a mere white place where you could project your movie. Instead, it was a multi-panel 4k LED screen that showed everything in ultra-sharp definition. It was amazing.

Instead of having a rack of DVDs, they had an automated rack of Blu-ray discs. It looked like a jukebox. You could flip, and then when you chose one of the discs, it would play that movie. It was absolutely awesome. I knew I would be back.

In the next room, they had a gym. It wasn't huge, but it had everything you needed. They had an elliptical, a treadmill, and a Stairmaster. They had racks of free weights and a complicated machine that had a set of instructions on the side for how to do a gazillion different workouts using it.

I went up to my room and put on a sports bra and running shorts. I laced up my sneakers. I grabbed my sports headphones and plugged them into my iPhone. I went downstairs to the basement, and I let the music take me away as I ran on the treadmill. I let go of all of the sorrow, all of the shock, all of the negative emotions from yesterday. My life was here, and now, in this gorgeous mansion with everything I would ever want and two handsome men who wanted me. Could life get any better than this?

I smiled as I thought about telling them tonight that I was fertile, that I was ripe for conception. Asher might be a gentleman about what it meant, but Xavier wouldn't be.

When I was done, my legs felt invincible, like they could go on forever. They were also sore. As I walked up the stairs, I was hobbling, using the stair rail for support. I went very slowly.

The housekeeper was already gone, and I walked upstairs to my room. She had cleaned up everything, and it sat in neat rows. My bathroom was far cleaner than I had ever made it.

I showered, getting the sweat off of my back. The water pressure felt great on my face, and I relaxed as the warm water flowed over me and my sore muscles.

I was just rinsing out my conditioner when my bathroom door opened. The shower door slid open. It was Xavier.

Fertile

"You're ready," Xavier said. He turned off the shower and pulled me into his arms. He kissed me thoroughly and fiercely.

"How did you know? I was going to tell you guys tonight."

"Honey, I'd have to be human-stupid to not smell you." I stiffened. "I'm sorry. I can smell. I have a nose." He tapped it.

Xavier picked me up off of my feet and threw me on my bed.

"There aren't time for niceties. Those will come later. Right now, I have to fuck you hard and fast."

He took off his clothes in record time. He discarded everything on the floor like it was trash, even though I could clearly see that his belt was Versace.

His body was magnificent, but not in the Mr. Olympia way. He was toned and broad-shouldered. It reminded me how Scotsmen threw trees. It was called tossing the caber. He looked like he tossed the caber every morning. I shivered in delight.

"Wait for me," came a voice over my shoulder.

Asher stood there, and he stripped just as fast as Xavier had. He had washboard abs and the same build as Xavier: huge, sturdy, and burly.

I was naked and wet in more ways than one. I readied myself as Xavier positioned his body between my open legs. He pushed them apart, far enough apart that my thighs protested.

"I'm going to fuck you until you can't walk."

Xavier pushed the tip of his cock against my wet opening, and I moaned. He rubbed my clit as he came in for a hard, brutal kiss.

He entered me with a hard, swift thrust.

It hurt. My body was not made to take someone as big as he was. I felt like my body was being torn into two separate pieces.

I whimpered.

Instead of stopping, the sound spurred him on. I breathed deeply as I adjusted to his size. The pain turned into hot pleasure coursing through my veins. It was a mix.

He pounded me with his big body overtaking my smaller, more delicate frame. He kissed me again and again, his tongue darting in and out with the rhythm of his cock. I arched my back and panted hard as I came, fluttering and milking his cock. He bellowed above me as he released spurt after spurt of hot seed inside of my body.

He collapsed on top of me, squishing me into a pancake. I liked it. Yeah, it was hard to breathe with his bulky form on top of me, but I ran my hands down his back. I liked his scent. It filled me and was all around me. Both of us fought to get breath back into our bodies.

After he caught his breath, Xavier levered his body off of mine, pushed off of his hands, and went off to the side.

Asher came to me. His eyes were filled with lust. They swept over my well-loved body. I felt like my limbs were weighted.

"You are going to ride me." In a half second, Asher was on the bed, lifting me above him for some acrobatic sex. My legs were straddling his body. My hair fell forward around his face, and I put it over one shoulder so it didn't get into his face.

"You know, this isn't the best position for conception."

"I don't care." Asher put his big hands on my hips. I had ample curves, but his size made me feel like I was just a tiny thing. He pulled me onto his hard rod, piercing my body. I gasped as he entered me. He was every bit as big as his brother, and I could only just barely take him. He forced me to take him a fast rhythm, because he pulled and pushed my body into place with his hands on my hips and his hard thrusts up. I could only hang onto his shoulders for dear life, grinding down on him when he pushed up inside of me.

My breasts were near his face, and he bit one, then licked the other. I moaned. He bit my cleavage. It hurt, but it felt good.

I turned my head so that I could bite his neck. He roared, and I felt his seed fill my body. It overflowed.

Xavier lifted me off of his brother, and he carried me with

just one arm into the shower.

Shower

"Have to get clean."

He pushed my back against the cool tile, which felt like a blessing after the burning passion we had all just experienced.

He turned on the water, then he took my bath gel and lathered up his hands. He cleaned up my neck, my arms, my tummy, and my legs. He turned me around to wash my back. I stood there, with my back to this beautiful man, and I shivered.

He bit the juncture of my neck and shoulder. I cried out from the fiery pain and pleasure radiating out.

He moved my legs so that my stance was wider. He knew what he wanted. I knew what he wanted, too, deep in my bones, in the most feminine part of me.

He pushed my body completely flat against the tile while he pushed his cock inside of my body. I moaned as I felt him stretch my small, tight pussy. He was rough with my body, pounding me against the tile. Unlike a bed, the tile didn't have any give. My body was trapped between his hard, muscular chest and the unforgiving tile. The water sprinkled down around us as he grunted and thrust into my body, pushing us closer to our peaks. I felt a warmth in my core. The warmth spilled everywhere in my body, and I gasped as I came.

When he felt me come, he used my body even more roughly. His hands were glued to my hips with enough force that I would have bruises for days. My feet were a foot off of the ground. He called out loudly behind me as he released his seed into my body. He let me go, and I slid down the tile.

Just as I got to my feet, Asher took Xavier's place. He spun me so that he could kiss me, possessing my mouth, branding me with his scent. He brought my arms up, and he collected my wrists in one gigantic hand. He watched the water make trails over my breasts. With my arms up, my breasts were thrust even closer to his face. He bit the top of my breast savagely, just at the line of where he would break skin. I moaned low in my throat, and he touched the line of my throat with his tongue, spreading hot fire where he touched me.

I saw his hand tugging on his dick, and he was fully erect. He guided his cock into my slit. Realizing that I was too short to take him like this, since I was more than a foot shorter than him, he lifted me. My legs went around his body. He let go of my hands, and they went around his neck. I was pinned to the wall by his big body. It was a position of extreme trust, because I could not move. Even though I had known him for a very short time, something inside of me found its mate inside of him and Xavier. He penetrated me, invading my body. He rolled his hips. My ass was pushed even harder against the cold tile. He surged forward and retreated. My pussy held him tightly, reluctantly letting him go. He bit my ear. I couldn't help myself. I yelled as I felt my orgasm take over my body. He was not far away, wildly pushing me into the wall, far beyond rhythmic pounding. He thrust deeper inside of my body. As I looked into his ferocious eyes, I knew that he was about to impregnate me. He roared loudly, staring straight into my eyes, as he spilled himself inside of my fertile body.

He pulled out of me, and he set me on my feet.

He sat down on a ledge. "My legs feel like jelly right now."

"Mine do, too." I straddled him and kissed him on his mouth. His hand came up to grope my breast.

"You're really perfect." He kissed my nose. "I can't think of a better mother for my child."

"I'm so glad that you're going to be a father." I kissed him lightly on his cheek, caressing the other one gently with my hand.

"How would you feel about a nap, hmm? I normally don't take them, but today might be an exception."

"Sounds great to me."

We soaped up and used the shower to rinse off. Instead of it being a sensual dance, it was more utilitarian now. He wrapped me up in a towel, and he dried off and then hung it up. Even when he wasn't erect, his dick was impressive.

He saw me looking. "I need to take a rest for now. But I'll give you some later. That's a promise."

He laughed when red touched my cheeks. "Come on."

He picked me up.

"You guys are always picking me up. I have feet, you know."

"I know." He kissed me. "But it's more fun like this. I love feeling your curvy body in my arms. I wish I could keep every luscious inch of you on my skin 24/7." He put me on the bed and climbed in after me. He settled behind me, throwing a heavy paw around my waist. I felt safe and secure as his whole body was wrapped around me. I fell asleep.

Jayce

When I woke up, I saw a credit card on my nightstand with a note. It said:

Hello, darling. I forgot to give you this earlier. We got distracted.

I grinned, thinking of the superb distraction.

Here's your credit card. We'll take care of your living expenses while you're with us. Go shopping this afternoon. Buy something sexy. We'll see you tonight. Come home after 5. Asher

I frowned. Why didn't they want me in the house until after 5?

I shrugged. I might as well go shopping. I was sure that my clothes were traumatized by being thrown on the street like that, and I knew that some retail therapy would perk me right up.

* * *

At 6 PM, I parked my car in the driveway and walked into the house. The house was full of people, very tall people, just like Asher and Xavier. I stopped in the kitchen, unsure if I should run for it.

"Hey, honey," Asher said. "There are some people I'd like you to meet."

"Jayce, Alex, Caleb," he pointed

to all of them in turn. "They are part of our sleuth."

"Sleuth?" My brow furrowed. "Like a detective? Like Monk?"

All four of them laughed. "No. A sleuth is the name for a group of bears."

I blinked. "Oh! That makes sense." I nodded to them. "It's nice to meet you."

The one closest to me sniffed. His face got inappropriately close to mine, and I heard Asher let out a growl. He ignored Asher and smelled me, practically putting his nose on my hair.

"You're pregnant."

Asher was still. "Are you sure?"

Jayce gave me a glare. I took a step back under the weight of his hatred. But it disappeared so quickly that I thought that I could have imagined it.

"Congratulations," he said, turning to Asher. "You and Xavier are going to be daddies."

"Thanks, man," Asher said stiffly. He put an arm around my shoulders and kissed my cheek. "I'm excited," he whispered in my ear. "Wait until they leave."

Alex and Caleb started coughing in a way that sounded suspiciously like laughing.

"We better go," Alex said. "Nice to meet you." He nodded at me, and I got the impression that he tipped his hat at me, although he didn't move his hand at all and wasn't wearing a hat. Caleb gave me a smile and a wave.

Jayce was the last to leave, his eyes bouncing around the kitchen.

"See you soon."

Asher picked me up. He kissed my cleavage. "I can't wait to see my son feed at your perfect tits."

"My body will be ruined by a baby."

A blaze of anger flashed on Asher's face. "Don't ever say that. Pregnant women are the most beautiful girls in the world." He smelled my hair. "He's right. You are pregnant. Funny how it took Jayce to notice."

"I don't think he likes me."

Asher shrugged, his arms bringing me up about a half inch more. "He is the one with the most to lose if we don't have a cub. He already has a mate, Melanie. She stays at home, taking care of their cub, Seth. If we didn't have a baby in the next two years..."

"He would take over your sleuth," I completed, gathering the pieces of the puzzle.

"He'll get over it," Asher said. "This sleuth has always been ours. Yeah, our dad was the head of the sleuth, but you get here by being the strongest fighters. Xavier and I have done a good job of leading our sleuth so far. This will just cement our leadership." He kissed my temple. "But enough about me. Right now, it's all about you."

"Where's Xavier?"

Asher smiled and walked up the stairs. "He's out taking care of something. Right now, I have you all to myself."

We were in his bedroom now. It was gray with accents of brown. I leaned up and kissed him. He sat on the bed, with me across his body. He took off my clothes reverently, as if I were made of glass. He kissed every bit of me that he revealed.

"You're unbelievably beautiful."

He stared into my eyes as we joined our bodies, his cock sliding into my soaking wet pussy. He set a slow, smooth pace for us. He rocked into my body with the motion of the ocean, and I closed my eyes. I was filled with peace and love, for Asher, our baby, and Xavier. It was all going to be good.

When our climaxes came, they weren't sharp and sudden. They were slow, welling up inside of us. I began to flutter, and he began to pulse inside of me. He kissed my eyes before he slowly filled me with his come. He pulled out of me and rolled to the side. I put my arm and top leg around him, and our faces were right next to each other on our pillows.

"I'm happy about the baby," I told him.

"I am, too."

He kissed my forehead. "Now rest. If you're pregnant with a baby bear, you better get some sleep."

I didn't know why I was tired all the time. It wasn't cold, so I couldn't be hibernating. But somehow, all my energy was gone. I nuzzled my face into his neck, and I was out like a light.

Staying In

When I woke up, I was still naked and in Asher's room. I felt between my thighs. I wasn't sticky, so he had cleaned me up while I was asleep. I picked up my clothes, and I went to my room to put on a new outfit. I put on a gray skirt with a chocolate-colored shirt.

I went downstairs and saw Xavier. He whooped and spun me around.

"Gentle!" Asher barked. "You asshole, she's pregnant."

"It's ok!" I said, seeing Xavier's

frown. "I'm not that delicate."

He kissed me, a big smacking kiss on my mouth, before he put me down again. "You're pregnant! This is the best news ever. Do you want to go out to celebrate?"

"No," I said, raising a single brow. "I'd rather stay in."

Xavier knew what I meant, and he gave me a very sexy lopsided grin.

"I think that could be arranged. I'll get a chef to drop by with the food already prepared, and we can...stay in."

He picked up his phone and texted someone.

"What are you doing?"

"Using Magic."

Was he a wizard? "What?"

"Magic," he said. "It's an app. You ask it for what you want, and they make it happen. I want a decent meal delivered in the next hour. They'll make it happen. They charge you extra if you need something fast but," and here he shrugged, "money isn't really a problem for us."

I looked at their expensive Bel Air mansion. "You can say that again. Your basement is insane."

He smiled at me, with genuine pleasure in his eyes. "You like it? I designed it."

"You designed it? It's

fantastic."

He looked at his watch. "We have some time. Do you want to watch a movie?"

"Okay." I touched his arm. "Lead the way."

Asher stayed upstairs while the two of us walked to the stairs.

He brought me down into the basement, and he headed in a beeline for the theater room.

"I'll set an alarm on my phone for 50 minutes. They'll ring the doorbell anyway."

"Shouldn't you be on the first floor to hear it?"

"Nah," he said, shaking his head. "The doorbell is part of an intercom system. It rings throughout the entire house."

He sat down and patted his lap. "Right here, girl. Got you the best seat in the house."

I sat on his lap timidly, at the very edge, near his knee. He pulled me back deeper, so that my back was touching his front.

"Better," he proclaimed. He picked up a remote from somewhere and started the movie.

I have no idea what went on in that movie. I knew that it was a James Bond movie featuring Daniel Craig and his incredible eyes. There was a female whose name I didn't catch. The movie was

Casino Royale, and there were random people with guns. At one point, James pulled out a gun from his sliding glove compartment, which I considered a safety hazard.

Mostly, though, my mind was on the scent of the man behind me. It was full, rich dark spice, better than anything you could buy from a store. He put his chin at the juncture of my neck and shoulder, and I could feel the abrasion of his beard.

Frankly, I did not know if he was paying attention to the movie, either. His hand crept between my thighs, and he eventually got impatient. Instead of rubbing my clit through two layers of clothes, he slid his hand under my skirt, under my skimpy panties, and right to my clit. I gasped quietly through a fast orgasm in front of him, wiggling. He withdrew his hand from under my skirt. I heard him unbuckle his belt and unzip his pants.

"Lean forward."

I put my legs on the outside of his, and I leaned forward. I had no idea what was happening on screen at this point.

He pulled my underwear to the side, and then he pulled my body down on his waiting dick.

"Uh," I grunted, as he filled me

up.

"So good," he panted behind me. He began crashing into me violently, with the force of a tsunami. He came fast, spilling inside of me. He kept his dick in place as he moved us over to the edge of the couch.

Before I could ask what he was doing, he took a tissue out of a box and as he pulled out, he wiped me up.

"Don't want to get come stains on your skirt," he told me.

"That's okay," I said, turning my face around so that I could see him. "It would be worth it." He kissed me hard and fast, and then he stood up, pushing me to my feet, too.

"As much as I want to spend the rest of my life down here with you, we better eat something." As if on cue, his stomach grumbled loudly. "I'll eat you later," he said, his voice growly and deep. I looked up at him and gave him a slow grin. He smacked my ass before he walked upstairs.

Dinner

As we got there, I saw Asher laying out more food.

"You horn-dogs," he joked, "leaving me up here to do all the work."

I could smell the delicious scent of fried chicken. It had always seemed to me like you could gain weight just from the smell.

"Are those blueberry waffles?" I said, confused. "Why are they blue?"

"They are blue corn waffles. They do come with a bourbon-berry compote, though." Asher spooned some of it on top of a blue waffle and gave it to me. "Try." I picked it up with my hand, careful not to get anything dirty, and I put the waffle in my mouth. I didn't know what to expect. It tasted really good.

"I think all waffles should be like this. Fluffy, light, perfect."

Asher bowed. "You're welcome."

"Whatever, asshole," Xavier snorted. "I ordered the chicken and waffles, not you."

"There's a chicken sausage and okra gumbo, too, if you want it."

"Yum," I said. "My grandma

was always feeding me okra when I was a kid. I haven't eaten it since she died."

I sat down with a juicy drumstick. The fried chicken was delicious and messy. There was something primal and satisfying about sinking my teeth into meat and ripping it off the bone.

The boys cleaned up, although they were careful to leave me enough food. Something about hanging out with them was making me ravenous. I wanted to eat maybe double what I normally would. I guessed that I was eating for two.

I took the plates to the sink

when we were done for the housekeeper to take care of tomorrow. The contrast of the sweet syrup and berry compote with the salty fried chicken was perfect. I somehow still had room for some of that gumbo. It warmed me in more ways than one.

This time, I cleaned up almost as much as the boys.

"You are eating way more than you were before," Asher said, pride showing in his eyes. "If we didn't know that our cub was inside of you before, we would know now."

I put a hand on my stomach, on my food baby. It did feel round and a little firmer than a food baby normally felt. It was if I were two or three months pregnant instead of just a day pregnant.

"I can't wait to have this baby."

I smiled at them. Both of their eyes blazed with desire as they looked at my pregnant body.

There was ringing through the intercom system.

Xavier was on his feet, ready to take the head off of whomever dared to disturb us just as we were going to get down to it.

"What?" he spat at the poor soul at the door. Probably an innocuous FedEx guy or something.

"I brought something for her,"

Jayce said. "I won't take up much of your time."

He walked into the kitchen. "I bought you prenatal vitamins and some Vitamin C."

"That's so thoughtful," I said. Asher and Xavier looked at each other.

"Yeah, thanks, man," Xavier said stiffly. "We'd like to fuck our mate now."

I gasped at his crude language, but Jayce only laughed. "Out." He waved, and he was gone.

"Don't touch those," Asher cautioned as soon as the door was shut. "We don't know what's in them. I'm going to send them to a lab that we use. The only prenatal vitamins that you are taking are ones that you personally are getting from a pharmacist."

"Don't be silly," I said. "Surely he wouldn't be desperate enough to give me something that would hurt the baby."

Xavier shook his head, and he squeezed my hand. "Never underestimate what a desperate man would do. We'll protect you from everything. It doesn't matter if it turns out to be harmless. I'd rather see shadows where there are none." There was a little bit of pain in his eyes.

"We'll just put these away,

then," I said, putting them away in a cabinet. "We'll get some prenatal vitamins soon."

I could see the relief on their faces, although I thought that their fear was unfounded.

I yawned.

"Go to bed," Asher said. "We've been wearing you out. We'll see you in the morning. Go."

I was too tired to protest. I went straight to my room and slept.

Hospital

I woke up in the middle of the night with my stomach telling me that I needed to hurl. I barely made it into the bathroom before I worshipped the porcelain god. I got vomit in my hair. I cried. I felt awful. I tried to get the vomit out of my hair. I was too sleepy to shower.

Careful not to make too much noise, because the boys were asleep in their own beds, I went downstairs and went to the cabinet. I knew that I had told the boys that I wouldn't take them, but prenatal vitamins helped with morning sickness, right?

I popped some Vitamin C and took one of the pills that Jayce had given me. Tomorrow, we'd pick up more prenatal vitamins. But for right now, these would have to do.

I went to bed after drinking a glass of water with the pills.

* * *

When I woke up, something was wet between my thighs. Oh, I started my period.

When I came fully awake, my eyes snapped open. I wasn't supposed to have my period. I was pregnant. I was miscarrying. Why had I trusted my midnight logic?

"Asher!" I screamed. "Xavier!"

They both came running into my room, both naked. They saw the blood that soaked my sheets.

"Oh my god!" Asher said. "We have to get you to a hospital." Xavier ran to his room to call, and I could hear his deep voice over there. Asher carried me into the bathroom, as if washing the bloodbath off of me could stop my body from losing our baby.

I cried, wailing loudly, and I could see the news hit Asher like a hammer.

He left me in the shower to go to my closet to get a dress. It was a simple black cotton one.

"I need to get a pad," I said. I wasn't ashamed right now. I was bleeding everywhere. I went to my suitcase, dripping some blood onto my carpet, and I tried not to be utterly devastated.

I put my pad in a set of my underwear, and I got dressed.

"Driving you to the hospital is going to be faster than waiting for an ambulance. Let's go." Xavier's car keys were in his hand.

We went to the hospital. The mood in the luxurious car was absolutely somber, like a black cloud had eaten us. I wasn't crying now. I just felt numb. How could I lose my baby so fast?

My beautiful baby.

Asher's arm was around me. Xavier was driving, while the two of us were in the back seat. I stared out the window in a haze.

When we got to the emergency room, they made me sit there and wait for a doctor. I told them that I was in the process of miscarrying, but they did not care. They wanted to see my insurance. I had only just gotten a policy, but Xavier and Asher had taken care of it. I sat there, feeling my body crumbling inside.

Finally, I got into an examination room. There was a nurse who took my vitals and an intake interview. Then, there was a doctor. I hated the sharp smell of the chemicals that they used in hospitals. The fluorescent lights were harsh, unflattering. I didn't want to be here.

"Let's see, hmm?" the doctor said. No hello, no how are you, no what's the problem. I was flat on the examination table as he checked my blood flow between my legs. "That does seem to be consistent with a spontaneous abortion."

"Abortion?" Asher asked. "It's a miscarriage."

"That's the medical terminology," the doctor answered

smoothly, calmly. He didn't give a damn about my baby. Our baby. Our cub. We were only a frantic trio of people marching into the ER looking for help. It didn't mean that we had to find it.

"There's nothing for it. Just wait it out."

"You can't save the baby?" I asked. "Please. I want this baby."

He shook his head. "It's already too far gone."

I barely noticed the tears running down my face. Xavier and Asher went to hold me. The doctor took off his latex gloves with a snapping sound and washed his hands carefully in the sink. "Go home."

Xavier took care of the money while Asher pushed me in a wheelchair back to the car. The nurses had not stopped him when he commandeered one. I was glad. I felt so fragile, like I was made out of ice that could melt or shatter at any second. I felt a deep, dark pit inside of me where a little life used to be.

Our car was dead silent as we drove home.

I went up to my room. I didn't want to talk to them. I didn't want to talk to anyone.

Asher came into my room. "Baby, it's ok. We'll have another

chance. You're young. Healthy. We can try."

I started sobbing, drinking in great gulps of air as I cried. He wrapped his big body around mine.

"It's my fault," I confessed. "I took one of those stupid pills that Jayce gave me. I thought they would help with my morning sickness."

I felt a jolt go through his body and looked up at his face. "Jayce did this?" His face settled in hard lines.

"Xavier!"

Xavier came into my room. His face was still and grim. "What is it?"

"It was those fucking pills," Asher said. "She thought they would cure her morning sickness."

"Oh, no," Xavier said. "We should have destroyed them as soon as their evil entered this house. I'll send them to the lab to get tested. I'll drive there now and be there when they open their doors." Xavier went back to his room and put on clothes. I could hear the jingle of his keys as he ran down the stairs to his car and the slam of the cabinet door where those accursed pills were.

I felt terrible. I turned to Asher. "You shouldn't have chosen me. I accidentally killed my baby. And for what? Just so that I would stop throwing up? I was already a terrible mother, so terrible that I killed my baby before it was even born." I buried my face in my hands.

"Shh," he said. "It's ok. Did you know a third of first pregnancies miscarry in the first trimester?"

I sniffled and looked up at him. "Really?"

"Yeah. It's your first baby. It's ok." He kissed my cheek. "You'll heal. It'll be fine."

My miscarriage lasted two days. Two long days of finding blood in the toilet. Two long days of beating myself up for being the worst. For being too stupid. For trusting that people were who they said they were.

The lab results were back. Jayce had given me something loaded to induce a miscarriage. I hadn't even cried when Xavier told me. I knew it in my heart that my baby was dead because of those pills.

* * *

I had been a zombie for a week when Xavier said something to me at dinner. We were eating boneless beef short ribs in a red wine sauce with broiled parmesan polenta.

"You're acting as if you're so sad. And you can be. But you

know, we're sad, too."

"Yeah, because your precious heir is gone and your leadership roles are in jeopardy," I snapped. "I lost my baby."

"It was our baby, too." Xavier's mouth had a mulish set to it.

Asher, ever the peacemaker, tried to defuse the tension. "Hey," he said. "We're all sad here. There's no need to bite each other, ok?" He put an arm around me and squeezed me tight. "I know that this has been hard for you."

I stood up, and I held out my arms to Asher. He picked me up and cuddled me.

"We'll be ok," Asher whispered

into my hair. "The three of us will be fine."

Our food was forgotten as Asher took me into his room.

Asher's Room

He undressed me slowly.

"Lean back," he said.

I leaned back, my legs at the edge of the bed.

He ate me slowly and carefully, starting with a circular dance around my clit. He tongued my pussy and used his fingers to touch my g-spot. I pushed up, and he licked me faster. My body came apart under him.

"Thank you," I said. "Would you like me to return the favor?"

"No," he replied swiftly. "Tonight was just for you. I'll take you back to your room. You don't have to do anything."

I looked at his face. He was such a good man, a kind one, and a gentle one. He was a true gentleman.

"I want to."

"Just go back to your room," Asher said, running his hand through his hair, making it stick up straight. "I don't want to do anything that you're not ready for."

"I am ready." I stood on the bed. Because his mattress was so expensive, luxurious, and thick, I was taller than him for once. I bent down to kiss him on the mouth. After a second of resistance, he kissed me back. I controlled his head with a hand at the base of his neck, fingers laced through his hair. I felt our connection reforming, our bond re-solidifying after the literal death blow.

"Can I come in?"

Xavier was hovering by the door. For the first time ever, I saw insecurity on his face. He was always so confident, so ready to take on the world. But he didn't know how to cure this, my sadness and his and Asher's from the loss of our baby.

"Yes," I said. I smiled even though my eyes were filled with tears. "Yes." We all needed to heal.

I got back on the bed, and I motioned with my hand for Asher to lay in front of me. He did, his body taking up the entire length of the bed. Xavier was behind me.

I was naked, and Xavier's hand massaged my ass then my clit, focused on my pleasure. Tonight was not about making a baby. It was about forging a connection between the three of us. Asher switched it up so that we could 69. He dove right back towards my pussy, and Xavier took his hand away from my clit. Asher's dick was in my face, and I sucked it down. I tugged on it with one hand and touched his balls with the

122

other. If the increased speed with which he licked my clit was any indication, he liked it. He tapped my thigh right before he flooded my mouth with his warm come. It was salty as I swallowed it down.

I didn't know where it came from, but Xavier had lube. It was cold and wet against my ass. He pushed a finger inside of me, pushing past my sphincter, getting me ready. I could hear him as he coated his dick with lubricant. He pushed it slowly inside of me. I had never had anal before. It felt different. I knew that Xavier wasn't here because I should be pregnant. He was here because he wanted me, and he wanted us to be ok. And it meant the world to me.

He came with a groan inside of my body, filling my ass with his come. It felt different from when he came in my pussy.

I felt good. I knew now that I wasn't just a baby-making machine for them, that they weren't just filling me with their come because they needed to have a child. They genuinely cared about me, and they cared about us. For the length of my stay in their house, we would be ok. All of us would be ok. I turned to Xavier, slipping his cock out of my ass, and I kissed him tenderly.

"Thank you," I said. "That was the nicest time I have ever had."

Xavier walked into the bathroom. I could hear the sound of running water. He came back into the room with two damp washcloths. One, he threw at Asher. The other one he used to clean me up. The warmth felt good on my body. Asher had always been the one to treat me lovingly, but now, as I looked up at Xavier while he cleaned my body, I knew that Xavier felt the same way about me as Asher did. It was written all over his face.

Even though all three of us had our own bedrooms, we stayed

there in Asher's gigantic California King bed. Xavier had an arm wrapped around my waist, and Asher's leg was around mine. I fell asleep, entangled in the two of them, safe and glowing inside.

That night was the dawn of a new era.

Job

The next morning, Asher talked to me as soon as I woke up.

"What do you want to do?"

I was touched. I wasn't some poor girl that they had picked up off the street anymore. Before, they had just left me at home to my own devices.

"I have to have a flexible job, of course, but I want to do something that helps other people."

"Like what?"

"How about a crisis pregnancy center?" I remembered how panicked the girls with whom I had grown up were when they realized they were pregnant. It didn't matter if you're raised in an upper class household if your parents throw you out without a cent. "Okay. I will fund whatever you want to do."

We started a crisis pregnancy center that I ran using their money. It felt good to help frightened teenage girls whose parents had kicked them out, and I secretly hoped that being around so many pregnant women would increase my fertility somehow. I didn't know how, but maybe there would be something in the air.

I filled my days, while Xavier

and Asher went away to do their mysterious work, with the logistics of running a large household that needed childcare. We had all-house classes on how to do things like figure out your finances and coordinate with other people. Since it was up to me, I was all for providing subsidized childcare for them even after they had their children and moved out. I could not keep all of them for life, because there were a limited number of bedrooms. What I could do for them was open up a daycare from 6 AM to 10 PM, which meant that they had more flexibility than a normal 9-to-5. There were a lot of mothers who were limited in their job choices by the cost of childcare, and I tried to fix that.

I had to coordinate food deliveries that were almost like food deliveries for a small restaurant. Pregnant women were hungry women. Pickles and ice cream might be cliché, but the joke existed for a reason. Our ice cream was constantly out, even though I increased our order every time.

I bought toys for the kids who would live there. I stocked up on carseats and strollers. It was fun to spend money this way, even more fun than spending money on myself when I went shopping. I was filled with a sense of purpose that guided me and drove me forward.

My days were busy, but my nights were even busier.

I had taken over ordering dinner, putting it on our house's tab. Asher and Xavier kept me up every night until the break of dawn. They were absolutely insatiable in the bedroom. I may have been walking around with dark circles under my eyes, but I was happier than I had ever been. I had a job that helped people. I had two gorgeous werebears making sweet love to me every night.

One day, I found myself in the

center's kitchen digging out a bowl of chocolate ice cream. I normally tried to keep it to a single scoop, but I found myself making a gigantic mound of ice cream in my bowl.

"Oh my god," Alison giggled, walking into the kitchen. "Save some for the rest of us!"

I blinked at my ice cream. I thought that I should stop by a pharmacy on the way home.

Pregnancy

I went to our local CVS, which was on the way home. I walked through the aisles, reading the signs, trying to find the pregnancy aisle. Did that even exist?

"Hi! How can I help you?" I saw a gangly, tall teenager with adolescent acne. He seemed nice enough, though.

"I'm looking for pregnancy tests."

I saw his eyes drift towards my stomach.

"Yeah, of course. They're over here."

He brought me to the aisle. The number of pregnancy test was dizzying. I didn't know which one to pick.

"Do you know which one I should get?"

He looked at me in shock. "Um...I've never had to buy one."

That at least made me smile. "Okay." I acted like it was Supermarket Sweep, grabbing one of every distinct kind that I could figure out. He helped me when the stack of pregnancy tests were overflowing. He took me straight to a cash register that was on the side of the store. It had a tiny counter instead of the broad counter up front, but I still didn't have to wait for a line of 10 people in front of me.

"So, did you find everything you needed?"

I looked at him. "Um, you helped me find everything."

"Sorry, I have to ask," he said, a tiny bit of pink touching his cheeks.

"Yeah, I found everything I needed." Or I would, as soon as I got home and peed on a stick. Well, a gazillion sticks.

I put it into the passenger seat of my car. The bags of pregnancy tests weighed enough that I had to buckle them in or the car would be annoying.

I drove home, nervous. The boys were home, and they saw that I had CVS bags in my hands.

"Why did you go to CVS? We could have sent the housekeeper."

"No, we couldn't have." I took a deep breath. "These are pregnancy tests."

The specter of the real reason that I was living in there house came back full force. Yes, we were pretending like I was actually their wife, living with them, sleeping with them, loving them. But I was there for a purpose.

"Do you need help?" Asher said. "You look a little shaken up."

"Nah," I said. "I'm going to go to my bathroom and check out these tests. I'll talk to you when I have a result, one way or another."

I walked upstairs with my bags of pregnancy tests. I drank some tap water. I should have had more water if I wanted enough pee for all of these pee sticks.

I ran out of pee when I got to my fifth one. The instructions said that I had to wait two to three minutes.

Those minutes felt like an absolute eternity. I looked at my phone, watching the seconds tick by more slowly than I had ever seen them go.

"Come on!" I urged my phone.

Xavier was in my doorway.

I was so embarrassed. I was sitting on my toilet with my pants down.

"Go away!"

"No," he told me. "This is my child, too."

The results started showing up on the pregnancy tests. I saw the pink lines and the indicators telling me one thing.

"I'm pregnant," I said, as I looked at test after test that said the same thing.

Xavier gave me a big hug. He kissed me quickly. "I'm so happy. Let's go tell Asher."

"Asher!" he yelled.

"Why are you yelling when we have an intercom system?"

He shrugged. "Because I can."

I heard Asher's heavy footsteps on the stairs. "What is it? What do the tests say?"

He looked at my happy face and Xavier's joy.

"We're having a baby!"

He picked me up, off my feet, and I was a foot off the ground as he kissed me.

"We won't tell anybody," he said. "We'll keep it a secret."

"How long am I going to be pregnant? The last time, I was instantly two or three months along with the baby."

"Were-cubs grow fast. That's why you needed so much food and so much energy. Bears in the wild take about 7 months, while humans take 9. Were-cubs take half that, about 3 months."

"Okay. What does this mean for my work?"

"You can't go out there," Xavier said. "It's too dangerous. What if you got in some kind of accident?"

I rolled my eyes. "I've been dealing with LA traffic my

entire life. I'm not afraid of accidents. And you can't imprison me on house arrest until the baby comes."

"How about this? Let's have a compromise. You telecommute for your job. We'll hire someone to be your on-the-ground coordinator. I have someone in mind."

"Already?" That was very fast.

"Yes." Asher nodded. "I know someone we can bring on. She's the wife of another member of the sleuth."

"Sounds good to me," I replied. "Let's do it."

The transition to bring on another managing director was absolutely seamless. That was great, because this time was just as hard on me as the first time. I had hyperemesis gravidarum. They didn't have to put me on house arrest. I was on hospital arrest. I couldn't keep anything down, not even water, which meant that they had to keep me hydrated with an IV drip. I hated it. I hated the smell of the hospital. The maternity suite that the boys paid for was baller and absolutely pretty, but I hated being bed bound, and I hated not being able to eat anything. I knew better than to resent the little one for what my body did, though. I was glad that I was telecommuting and able to take my mind off of being trapped in this hospital bed in Cedars-Sinai. Kara and I texted every day, and she and I Facetimed at night. She worked odd hours because of her job. Life was okay, though sort of quiet and slow. Inside of this hospital, my life was on pause.

Then, I felt my water break.

Delivery

It felt like someone had popped a water balloon between my legs. The wetness gushed between my legs, and I was soaked. I rang the call button to tell the nurse. She came running, which was good.

"My water just broke," I told her. "I'm having a baby!"

As a seasoned maternity nurse, she kept cool.

"Okay. Let me know when your contractions are coming less than a minute apart. I'll tell the doctor. Do you have anyone you want to contact?"

"I'll call Asher and Xavier myself." I couldn't feel anything, not a single contraction, nothing. "I'm sure they'll be here right away."

They must have basically teleported, because they were in Cedars-Sinai almost before I ended the call.

"How are you feeling?" Asher said. He took my hand and squeezed it.

"I feel okay." I shrugged. "This doesn't feel painful."

Xavier said, "You don't look like those women in the videos that we had to watch for preparation. You look almost normal, although you're ready to pop. I'm going to get the nurse."

Xavier went out to get the nurse. The nurse came into my hospital room, and she checked my vitals.

"You know what sometimes helps? Walking. I would never leave you to do it unsupervised, but the two of them should be able to keep you healthy and safe." She took our menage relationship in stride, just as the entire hospital staff had. Unconventional relationships didn't matter if you had enough money.

"Why don't you walk around the unit? There's a purple stripe that runs all the way around. It makes a square. Just tell me when you can feel the contractions coming less than a minute apart, ok?"

I nodded. She took the IV out of my arm. With the baby about to come out, it didn't matter that I wouldn't be hydrated by it. I hoped that the nausea and all-day sickness would recede once I delivered the baby.

I felt weak, since they only let me up out of my bed for an hour a day. It stunk to be on bedrest.

My werebears stood on either side of me as I swept around the unit, dodging women in wheelchairs, anxious fathers, busy nurses, and extra-busy doctors.

I followed the purple stripe around and around. The men were absolutely patient about it.

On the millionth round, my nurse looked at us and frowned.

"How fast are your contractions coming?"

"I don't feel anything."

"If you don't give birth naturally, we're going to have to induce labor. The risk of infection is too high. Let's hook you up and see what's going on in there."

I followed her back to my suite, and she had me lean back before she checked me.

"You're fully dilated," she said, confused. She hooked me up to a machine that counted my contractions. It spiked like crazy, as if my tummy was having a heart attack.

"Oh my god!" She rang some kind of emergency bell that brought nurses and doctors into my room on the double. "She's having a baby! Right now!"

There was a mad scramble around me to get everything in place. The doctor stood by. I didn't really feel anything still.

"Push," the doctor told me.

"Push," the nurse said.

"Push," everyone everywhere

said. I pushed.

"The baby's crowning."

Xavier and Asher's faces were completely white.

With another hard push, the baby came out, covered in placenta. The nurse whisked my baby away to clean her up, and the doctor tested her Apgar score.

From the volume coming from her lungs, I knew that she was healthy.

I rested in my bed. The nurse brought my baby back into the room, and she put the baby at my breast. I had seen enough videos on how to nurse that I could help my baby latch on to me. The baby sucked at me until her little eyes drooped. While she nursed, the nurse asked me for the name. We had already agreed to put Asher's name on the birth certificate. He was far more likely to be patient if he got called in the middle of a school day to pick up our little Celeste. She fell asleep quickly. I took her off of me and handed her to Asher.

"Look at her."

"She's the most perfect thing in the world," Asher said. There were tears on his cheeks. "She is so beautiful, just like her mother."

"Tiny, too." Xavier took the baby from Asher. "She's the size of my hand, almost. I'm going to take her to the nursery." He brought her to the nursery, where the nurses would take care of her in a little warm crib.

When the baby was gone, I cried. They were happy tears, because my newborn baby was the light of my life. But I was also terribly sad, because this meant that I wouldn't see Asher and Xavier every day anymore. I hadn't spent a full year in their house. I wouldn't be their live-in lover anymore. I was just the mother of their child, seeing them on alternate weekends. Xavier came back into my room.

"I guess I have to move out now," I said softly. "Most of my stuff is in here, but I still have some of my things in your house."

"Move out?" Asher asked, absolutely horrified.

"You're not moving out," Xavier said with absolute conviction. "No way."

"You can see the baby anytime you like," I offered. "You said that you would buy me my own house. That was part of the bargain. I was going back to school, remember?"

"No," Xavier said. "We have a new bargain. You live with us. You stay with us. From the first moment Asher met you, he knew you were our mate. And I knew it, too. I could smell it."

Asher was looking sheepish. "We knew you were pregnant again before you did."

"You did?" I blinked up at him. "Oh. You could smell it. Why didn't you tell me?"

"We wanted you to find out on your own. We weren't sure how you would react."

I felt like there was a sun rising behind my breastbone. "So you don't need me to move out?"

"No. Definitely not." Xavier kissed me. "You should be with us forever."

I liked the sound of that.

But then I heard an alarm go off.

Kidnapping

"What is it?"

Asher was out the door before I finished my sentence. I could hear his footsteps as he ran down the hallway. He was back in my room in a half minute, breathing hard from sprinting.

"Someone took a baby."

There was a terrible sense of foreboding in my chest. I knew which baby it would be.

"Son of a!" Xavier said. I was trying to break him of swearing before the baby came.

"I think it's Celeste," I said,

crying.

"No," Xavier said. "It can't be, right? Where's the security in this place?"

Asher went out of the room. In another minute, he walked back into the room slowly. "Celeste is gone."

Xavier punched the wall.

"You're hurting your hand." I said numbly. "We have to find my baby."

"Our baby," Xavier said grimly. "Ours."

We knew who had taken her, but we had no idea where she had been taken. She was so helpless and vulnerable. Our baby had been safe and secure, but now she was taken by a shepherd to a hill where the wolves would eat her. Or bears.

"Find our baby," I said. "You have to find her."

Xavier was texting on his phone. "I already have a private investigator on it. The hospital has reported the kidnapping to the police."

"When did you notice the baby was gone?"

"When the alarm went off. She had been in the nursery for only a minute."

"And she, this Celeste, was just born, correct?"

"Yes," I confirmed, crying a little bit. I couldn't stop the tears from leaking from my eyes. "She was born less than 2 hours ago."

"Do you have anyone who would want to take the baby?"

"Jayce," Asher said like a curse word. "It had to have been Jayce."

"We played back the security tapes. It looks like it was a woman. Dark hair, looks a lot like her but older."

"My mom?" I said. My eyes widened. "Are you saying my mom stole my baby?"

"I'm not saying anything," the policeman said piously. "But we did make a printout."

He gave me a black and white still from the cameras. I felt everything drain from my face.

I turned over in bed and buried my face in my pillow.

"I guess that's a positive identification, then?"

"Yeah," Xavier said grimly. "I would say so."

The policeman must have picked up on the dangerous undercurrent in Xavier's voice. He was like a volcano about to explode, growling sub-vocally.

"We'll be in touch when we have more information."

They left us alone after Xavier growled at them.

I fell asleep. The birth and the kidnapped newborn were devastatingly tiring. I had a nightmare that my baby was gone, and I had to walk around an empty wasteland to find her. I went around and around and around, but I couldn't see her. I could hear her frantic screams. I knew she was there, and it hurt my heart to listen to her, knowing that she was being hurt, knowing that she was in pain. I eventually found her, like the Lindbergh baby, with a skull fracture. There was blood under her head, the precious, soft head that I had held in my arms for far too short of a time. I cried in my dream.

Crib

When I woke up, the first thing that I saw was a crib in my room. How could anybody be so cruel as to put a crib in my room when my baby was gone?

I heard a wail coming from inside of the crib.

"Oh!" I said. Little Celeste was in there, in a little onesie, under a precious pink blanket. She had a bow in her hair.

"How?"

I looked around, and Asher was dozing in a chair in the corner. His eyes came open.

"Oh, good! You're up."

"Where was the baby?"

He frowned. "It was your mom. Honestly, the security in the maternity ward is abysmal."

"My mom? I don't even talk to her."

"Yeah, I know. But Jayce knew that you were pregnant because he never saw you again."

"I thought that you guys were taking care of him after we found out what was in those pills."

Asher shook his head. "He said he had gotten them from someone else. While we had proof that the pills were to blame, we couldn't prove that he had made them or intended to hurt you."

"Oh. So he was still around."

"Was is the operative word."

"Did you kill him?"

I looked at Asher's eyes. He looked steadily back at me. "Oh." I knew the answer.

"The nurses let your mom in. She had your birth certificate and her ID to prove that she was your mom. No normal person would be that prepared, but she had been paid by Jayce to take the baby."

"Did she know that the baby was going to be killed?"

"No, he spun her a story that he had been in love with you and knocked you up. But then, apparently, the two of us stole you and trapped you in our house and this hospital."

"That's absurd. Don't you think that the nurses would notice if I had been kidnapped?"

"Your mom was too gullible. She wanted to believe him. He was throwing money at her, money to pay her rent and feed her alcoholism."

"Where's my mom? You didn't hurt her, did you?"

"She's in rehab. They're also putting her through grief counseling. She's not the first person to lose her spouse, you know."

I nodded. "I hope that we can have a relationship one day."

Asher sighed. "Maybe one day I can forgive her for nearly getting her granddaughter murdered."

He came to my bed.

"Kiss, please."

He kissed me, then he turned and put Celeste on my tummy.

I stared into her big eyes. "Are you hungry, precious? Mommy will feed you." I undid my gown so that she could latch. She sucked while staring into my eyes. I was happy to meet her when she was born, but I was even happier to have her back.

"No one will ever steal you

again," I swore. "No one will ever hurt you."

Asher nodded. "She'll be the most protected child in Los Angeles. No, the world. We'll make sure that she is never harmed by anybody."

Home

The next day, the baby and I were in good enough condition to get out of the hospital. They insisted on wheeling me out, although I was perfectly capable of walking. I swore to myself that I would walk for an hour a day now. I had rolled around in bed so I didn't get bedsores, but it wasn't the same thing as being healthy and moving around.

The boys had set up a huge nursery for our baby. We had three nannies, one per 8-hour shift, but they barely had to lift a finger. I spent all my time with my baby, utterly entranced by her sweet little eyelashes and her rosebud mouth. While she was nursing, she needed me.

When she was 6 weeks old, I went back to work via telecommuting. I found that the managing director that the boys had found had completely run things in my absence. I turned everything over to her, and I relaxed completely. I spent my days playing with my little one. I was delighted when she was strong enough to roll over and hold her head up. She was a precocious little girl, getting stronger far faster than a human baby would.

One night, I woke up to a scream.

Terrified that someone had stolen her, I ran to the nursery. There was a baby bear cub in her crib.

I guessed that the boys hadn't told the nannies what kind of household this was.

"Shh, it's ok," I said. We were going to have to send her to counseling.

Xavier and Asher came in.

"Wow! This is early for this kind of thing." Asher picked up our little cub and cuddled her, rubbing her tummy. She snarled at him, showing her little teeth. Instead of the few teeth that she should have had as a human baby, she had a full set of teeth.

For the first time, I saw my bear-mates shift. It was instantaneous. One moment, they were hot men, billionaires in Zegna suits. The next, the suits were shredded, and there were two enormous bears in the nursery.

The nanny fainted quietly in the corner. We would be paying a lot for her therapy.

The little baby cub, now on the ground, scampered through the house. Someone had opened the door to our back patio, and she ran out there. If she were a human baby, I would be terrified for her on the stairs. She wasn't strong enough.

As a bear cub, she confidently trotted down the steps and headed for a swim in the outdoor pool, which was bigger than the indoor one.

My heart was in my mouth as I watched her paddle around in there, and her fathers joined her, splashing around, having fun. I knew they would keep her from drowning.

This was not the kind of family scene I had never imagined for myself, but I was happy. I had a healthy baby and two loving fathers. Our family was safe and secure.

THE END

This is a work of fiction intended for mature audiences only. Names, characters, places, and incident either are the product